PUREST EMOTION

VOLUME 1

KOYIDALA SATISH

Made with ♥ on the Notion Press Platform
www.notionpress.com

"I dedicate this book to the persons who has been instrumental in shaping my perspective and enabling me to see the world through a different lens. Their guidance and encouragement have been invaluable, and without their influence, this story may never have been told. To them, I am forever grateful."

Contents

Preface

PREFACE

Ah, my dear readers, let me share with you a tale of how the smallest of incidents can have the most profound consequences. In this story, a single misstep sets off a chain reaction of events that spiral out of control, leaving lives in ruin and relationships in shambles. It's a cautionary tale of how one moment of carelessness can lead to a lifetime of regret. So hold on tight, my friends, as we journey through the twists and turns of this tale, and see how even the tiniest of actions can have the greatest of impacts.

Acknowledgements

ACKNOWLEDGEMENTS

I would like to express my deepest appreciation and gratitude to the following individuals, who have provided invaluable support and guidance throughout the writing of this book.

Firstly I would like to thank Chodi Santosh and Bandi Divya, whose insightful comments and constructive feedback have been instrumental in shaping the direction and focus of his work.

And last, but certainly not least, my warmest thanks to Chodi Umamaheswari, Narapareddy Satish , Pypuri Vijaya durga whose keen eye for detail and tireless efforts in proofreading and editing have significantly improved the clarity and coherence of this work.

CHAPTER ONE

Listen closely, my friends, and let me tell you a tale that will chill you to your very core. For it is a tale of darkness, of shadows, and of the unknown.

Picture this: Ram, a young boy, was fully engrossed in the latest horror movie on TV .Little does he know, he's about to find himself in the middle of his own spine-chilling tale. His piece is soon shattered, when his mother, Rekha, stormed into the room and demanded that he turn it off and finish his homework. Ram grudgingly turned off the TV and sat down at the table, to complete his homework. But as he began to work, he felt an eerie presence in the room, as if he was being watched by something sinister.

A child frightened by a mere horror movie is a common occurrence, but the possibility of a real supernatural presence lurking in the shadows is an intriguing prospect indeed.

He couldn't shake of the feeling of unease, and every time he looked up from his notebook, he felt like something was moving in the shadows .He tried to ignore the feeling and focus on his work, but the fear continued to built within him.

Suddenly, his notebook was pulled out of his hand and dragged into the darkness. Ram sat there, frozen with fear, as he watched in horror as his notebook was thrown back at him with his homework mysteriously completed.

A ghostly presence completing his homework? Oh, how convenient! I could have used such a presence when I was a student, although I would have preferred it to write my essays and take my exams for me.

And as for the identity of this malevolent force, who knows? Maybe it's just a mischievous spirit with a penchant for education. Or perhaps it's something more sinister, like my dear sister Haritha on a particularly bad day.

Ram couldn't explain what had just happened, and the fear inside him grew stronger. Ah, it seems that Ram's troubles were far from over. He tried to rationalize it, thinking that maybe it was just his imagination. But he couldn't ignore the nagging feeling that something was wrong. That night, as he went to bed, he couldn't shake off the feeling of unease that settled in his chest.

He tossed and turned, unable to sleep, as he heard strange sounds and whispers in the darkness. Ram eventually drifted off to sleep, exhausted from the events of the night. But his sleep was soon interrupted by the sound of a sheep bleating outside his window.

He got up to take a look and saw a helpless baby sheep that had fallen into a deep pit. Being the kind-hearted soul that he is, Ram doesn't hesitate to run outside and save the poor animal from harm.As Ram lifted the baby sheep from the deep pit, he suddenly felt a strange sensation. It was as if something was pulling him down, deeper and deeper into the ground. In a moment of confusion, Ram lost his grip on the sheep, and it disappeared from his hands into the darkness.Was this the end for poor Ram? Would he be swallowed up by the quicksand, never to be seen again?

In the distance, he saw a women with long, unkempt hair, calling out to him with her hand. He managed to break free and started walking towards the mysterious women.

He couldn't resist her allure and started walking towards her.

Despite his reservations, he continued to follow her, and soon found himself standing in front of an abandoned, decrepit house. In the torch light, all he see are shadows dancing. The darkness seems to be alive with their movement, as they twist and turn, constantly shifting in shape and size. And yet despite his fear, he cannot look away from the hypnotic spectacle before him.

The house was filled with a thick, eerie silence that seemed to press down on him from all sides. And yet, he couldn't help but be drown into its depths, following the women he had seen as she led him through the shadows. But as he searched for her, the women vanished into thin air. Ram was left alone in the darkness, surrounded by the ghostly whispers of the house.

You see, you've wandered into my domain, and I don't take kindly to intruders." said the ghost

Ram's mind was racing, trying to figure out how to escape this haunted house and the clutches of the ghost that had trapped him here. As he looked around frantically, he realized that the doors were locked and there was no way to go. The ghost began to crackle, and the sound echoed through the empty halls.

I have been waiting for someone like you, for a very long time, said the ghost.

"Please, let me go!" Ram pleaded, his voice trembling.

"I'm afraid it's too late for that," You can't escape from me, the ghost hissed.

Ram's knees trembled as he tried to take a step forward, but his legs wouldn't move.

"Mortal, you are in my territory, " the ghost hissed. The ghost continued to speak, her voice growing louder and more menacing.

I have been trapped in this mirror for centuries," the ghost continued. " And now , I need a friend to stay with me for eternity."

Ram felt a cold sweat break out his forehead, as he realized the gravity of the situation. He was stuck here, with a ghost that had been trapped in this house for centuries. He had to find a way out, and fast. As he looked around the room, he saw the ghost begin to move closer to the mirror. It's form twisted , and her eyes glowed a sticky green.

"But the ghost wasn't finished with him yet. " You see, mortal, I have a little proposition for you. Help me, and I'll let you go. Refuse, and, well... let's just say you won't like the consequences ", Your's only chance to escape is to listen to my story," the ghost said. Her voice now a whisper.

" But be warned , if you fail to answer my question , you will be trapped in this mirror with me for all eternity ,".

What is your story? Ram asked, his voice shaking.

Ah, my dear, you are in for a treat. The story I have to tell you is not for the faint of heart, but I can see that you are a true thrill-seeker, just like me. And with wicked grim, the ghost began to tell it's story .

CHAPTER TWO

THE STORY

My name is Sweety, as a young girl of five I have a great love for listening to stories. But let me ask you this, my dear. Are you ready for a tale that will chill you to your very core? A story that will keep you up at night. Picture this, my dear. A train journey to Manali, with crisp winter winds blowing and adventure awaiting at every turn. The perfect setting for a story, that will make your blood run cold, wouldn't you say?

And as luck would have it, I heard a tale that held me spellbound, with unexpected twists and terrifying surprises. Oh, how I relish those moments when a story takes hold of us, leaving us gasping for breath and unable to look away.

Allow me to transport you to another world, to experience things we never thought possible. And now, my dear friend, it's time for me to transport you to that world. Let me weave a tale that will make your skin crawl, your heart race, and your mind reel with terror. Are you ready to be truly frightened? And so, my dear, I leave you with this warning: be careful what stories you listen to on a dark and desolate train. You never know what horrors they may unleash.

CHAPTER THREE

THE JOURNEY

As the train chugged through the dark I sat at the window, gazing out the window into the inky blackness of the night. The rhythmic chug of the locomotive had lulled me into a drowsy state and my eyelids began to drop. It's dark, like really dark. The kind of dark that makes you feel like you're in a void. But I'm not scared, no. I'm sweety I don't get scared easily. My dad's with me, though. He is sleeping like a baby next to me.

The rhythmic sound of the train is making me drowsy. It's like a lullaby, you know? And before I know it, I'm nodding off. But I can't help peeking out the window. It's like I'm waiting for something to happen. Something to jump out of the darkness and surprise me.

Suddenly, out of nowhere, I see this huge, massive thing moving along with the train. I'm talking big, like really big. It's enough to make your heart skip a beat. I turn to my old man for some reassurance, but he's snoring away like nothing is going on.

I panicked a little. What if this huge thing comes back? What if it's dangerous? So I shake my dad awake and tell him what I saw. He's disoriented, but he manages to look outside. And just like that, the thing is gone.

But I know what I saw. And I can't tell the feeling that there's something out there, something that's not quite right. I keep looking out the window, waiting for it to come back. But it doesn't.

"I saw something dad, I swear!" I said. My mind still reeling from what had just happened.

Trying to shake off the unease I asked my father to take me to the restroom, but the washroom is occupied.

My father knocked the door, his voice was polite but urgent. "Hello? Can you make it quick? "

In response, there was a loud bang from inside of the restroom. My father recoiled, his heart shaking. "Okay, okay, take your time I'll use the other restroom", said my father.

I used the opposite restroom, and when I came out and walking back, like a mirage in the desert, I saw my grandmother emerged from the other restroom. I rushed towards her and hugged her, relieved to see a familiar face.

My father realized that the person who had banged in the restroom door was his mother-in-law. He was too scared to ask her about it, but he knew that something strange was happening.

My heart was racing as I sat back down in my seat, feeling like I couldn't trust my own eyes. The train continued to rumble down the tracks, it's been a while, i couldn't sleep and i couldn't stop staring out of the window. The occasional lights of passing town did little to assuage my anxiety.

I gently shook my granny's shoulder and said, "Granny wakeup. Can you tell me a story?"

But Granny was aware of the time and the need for the rest." Sweety it‘s late now. Let's hear a story in the morning, close your eyes and go to sleep", she said.

"Sweety, you need to keep your mouth shut and go to sleep right now!

One more word out of you, and I'll make sure you lose your teeth." said my mother.

I pretended to drift off to sleep, but as soon as my mother was out of sight, i couldn't help but open my eyes and whisper into my Granny's ear with my signature charm.

"Granny, my dear," i said, my voice dripping with honeyed sweetness. "Please do tell me a story. Just one, won't you?"

Granny couldn't resist my persuasive charm and began her narration , but I quickly grew bored with the predictable story. "No, no, no," i interrupted. "I don't want to hear about a regular father and his seven valiant sons. Boring!"

Granny smiled indulgently at my impatience. "Alright, my dear," she said, charmed by my enthusiasm. "Let me tell you the tale of a hero."

My eyes lit up at the mention of a hero. "A hero!" I exclaimed eagerly, my charm fully on display.

Granny couldn't help but chuckle at my excitement. "Not your typical superhero, sweety," she cautioned with a smile. "This is a hero of nature."

I settled back into my seat, intrigued by Granny's promise of a different kind of hero. "Go on," i urged, flashing my winning smile. "I'm all ears."

CHAPTER FOUR

THE VALIENT

Greetings, I am a hero of nature. I was not like any other hero's, I had a unique gift: i could sense the suffering of nature. While some humans may blame me for reducing the population, they often overlook my efforts in reducing pollution.

PLANET I N PERIL:

Once upon a time, in a far-off galaxy, there was a magnificent planet called Barth. It was a place of great beauty with rolling hills, sparkling oceans and teeming forests. But beneath its surface, the planet was in peril. Pollution and over population was taking a heavy toll on the environment, and the animals and plants that lived there were struggling to survive. The future of the planet was uncertain, and the humans who lived on it seemed unaware of the danger they were in. As I watch the devastation unfold, i couldn't help but feel a sense of concern. It's tragic to see the beautiful planet Barth being destroyed before my eyes.

But one day, I emerged from the depths of nature, to restore balance. I was a being with immense power, but also gentle and wise. And so, with a heavy heart, i decided to do what was necessary. I knew that many would condemn me for my actions, but I stand by them. Sometime's, the most difficult decisions are the right ones, and i will do whatever it takes to ensure the survival of life in the universe.

Initially people were frightened of me and labelled me as Bovid-19, and saw me as a threat to their very existence, resulting in hatred and fear. But slowly people began to understand that they were not above nature, but a part of it, and they needed to live in harmony with the Barth.

And you know what? They did it. They saved their planet. As the humans learned more about me, they began to see me in a new light, they realized that I am not a virus to be feared, but a hero to be celebrated. They worked together to find solutions to the challenges they faced, and they were amazed by the positive results. The once polluted skies were now clear and the animals and plants that lived on earth were thriving once again.

But the victory was bittersweet, for I knew that it had come at a great cost. I had been forced to make difficult choices, to sacrifice the few for the many, and it weighed heavily on my heart.

As I gazed out into the universe, I knew that there were other worlds like Barth, other worlds in need of my help. And I also knew that I would never again be able to turn a blind eye to the destruction wrought by those who would place their own desires above the needs of the planet. But even as I prepared to continue my work, I couldn't help but feel a sense of sadness for all that had been lost.

As the sun set on another day, I looked down on the planet with pride, knowing that I had helped to create a better future for all. The humans had finally understood that they were not above nature, but a part of it and they had learned to live in harmony with the Barth. The planet was once again a place of great beauty and vitality, and the future was bright.

Today I am honored to share with you an intriguing story of love, retribution, and the power of a kiss. This is a tale unlike any other, one that holds within it, the ability to transform the course of human lives and events.

As a humble participant in this story, I played a small yet significant role.

The wisdom of ages teaches us that when our motives for revenge are rooted in sincerity, nature will always provide us with the necessary tools to achieve our goals. Today, I have the privilege of narrating to you how I able to harness the power of a kiss to assist a human in their quest for revenge.

This is a story of passion and determination of a unwavering will of the human spirit and the incredible influence that a simple act can have on the world around us. So, sit back, relax and allow me to transport you to a world where love and vengeance collide.

CHAPTER FIVE

THE VICTORY

November 2019

The train whistle echoed through the station, signaling the start of the journey that will change three lives forever. Surya, Arjun and Laxmi were three school children with a passion for art. They were travelling with their teacher on a train to participate in a painting competition.

Surya has been working hard on a picture of a beautiful girl, while Arjun and Laxmi had been inspired by the stunning scenery they saw from the train window and decided to paint it together. It's always fascinating to see the different ways that people are inspired by the world around them.

But it's not just art that these three are focused on, oh no. They're also quite the entertainers, cracking jokes and performing acts of kindness and chivalry to impress their teacher and laxmi. I can't say I blame them, a little bit of charm can go a long way, especially when it comes to getting ahead in life.

Despite the fact that they're running late for the competition, it seems that they're all having a great time together. Sometimes the journey is just as important as the destination, and it seems like these three are making the most of every moment.

The teacher was thrilled to see the children playing and enjoying themselves. Despite the lateness, she was glad that, they were making the most of the journey. As they reached, teacher kissed Arjun and wished them all good luck for the competition. But little did she know that a single kiss would change the course of the story.

Suddenly, Arjun started feeling drowsy and cold.

Excellent, where were we? Ah yes, poor Arjun feeling drowsy and cold. It's always a concern when someone falls ill, especially in the midst of a competition, I suggested him to take some rest but as it is common with humans, he didn't listen to my words. Sometimes humans refuse to listen to good advice, even when it's coming from a hero like me with vast knowledge and experience .

Ah, it seems our trio of young artists has reached their destination, their paints and brush in hand, each determined to create a masterpiece that would astound the world.

Ah, the world of art. Such beauty and passion. The painting competition was underway, and the children were eager to showcase their talents. It was a delight to see such youthful enthusiasm and creativity on display.

As the competition, the children eagerly took their places and began to paint. Surya's brush flowed across the canvas, bringing his vision of the beautiful girl to life. Arjun and Laxmi worked together, capturing the essence of thescenerythey had seen from the train.

But as fate would have it, things don't always go according to plan. Arjun's health takes a sudden turn for the worse, leaving him unable to complete his portion of the painting. And in a fit of frustration, Revathi destroys their joint effort, leaving the two of them without a viable entry. It was a devastating turn of events, and my heart goes out to those young artists.

Despite these setbacks, the competition went on, and the judges ultimately declared Surya the winner with his stunning depiction of the beautiful girl.

As the train return to home, Surya displayed his newly won painting to a fellow passenger on the train, basking the euphoria of the victory.

However, his joy was short lived as laxmi emerged from the restroom with a sullen expression, belying the storm of emotions that raged within her, and my heart went out to her.

Despite her defeat, Surya welcomed her with open arms, offering her his medal in a gesture of love.

"Thank you, Thank you so much", said Ram.

But laxmi approach was far from what Surya has anticipated. Her jealously and anger simmered just below the surface, and she slowly approached him, planting a kiss on his forehead that was filled with conflicting emotions. She whispered a sarcastic "congratulations" in his ear and began to sensually run her fingers through his hair.

Laxmi's eyes narrowed, You don't deservethis," she hissed gesturing to the painting and medal. You don't deserve any of it.

Surya completely unaware of Laxmi's true intensions, asked her what she meant. But before he could even finish his sentence, Laxmi's anger boiled over and she pushed him out of the moving train with all her might.

As Surya's body tumbled and twisted on the tracks below, he heard Lakshmi's voice ringing in his ears.

The impact was devastating, and Surya's lifeless body lay on the tracks. As he crushed on the tracks, pain shot through his body, but it was nothing compared to the agony in his heart. His mind was filled with confusion and despair as he struggled to understand why she had done this to him.

Surya's heart was pounding in his chest as he struggled to comprehend what had just happened. One moment, he was celebrating his victory, and the next he was hurtling towards his death. The wind rushed past his ears as he trumbled helplessly through the air, his mind was consumed by the thoughts of the girl he loved.

He felt a deep sense of loss and regret, knowing that he would never know what it was like to hold her in his arms, to tell her how much he loved her.

In his last moments, Ram's thoughts turned to the painting that had brought him so much joy. It was a portrait of laxmi, painted with all the love he had for her. He had poured his heart and soul into it, hoping that it would express the depth of his feelings for her. And now, it was all he had left.

As his life slipped away, Ram clung to the image of laxmi in his mind, holding onto his love for her even as it brought him to his death. He felt a sense of peace wash over him as he released his final breath, knowing that his love would live on, even in the phase of such tragedy.

Surya thought he had won it all - the medal, the painting, and the heart of the woman he loved. But what he didn't know was that jealousy and anger can be powerful motivators, simmering just below the surface.

CHAPTER SIX

THE UNINVITED GUEST

The city was shrouded in darkness, a thick blanket of silence settling over the Sleeping metropolis .The only sounds that echoed through the air were the occasional barking of stray dogs, their howls piercing the stillness of the night . Then I noticed a lone figure staggering towards a house. As the figure drew closer, it became clear to me, that it was a man.

It was evident that he was drunk, his hand gripping tightly onto a bicycle for support.

Despite his inebriated state, he seemed determined to reach his destination. His movements were uncoordinated and haphazard, and I couldn't help but wonder if he was going to make it safely.

Finally, after what seemed like an eternity, he crashed the front gate of the house, his bike clattered to the ground, he pushed to open the gate and stumbled towards the door.

With a newfound sense of boldness, the man banged on the door continuously, his drunken state amplifying his persistent demands for entry. But no one answered .Just as he was about to give up, the door creaked open revealing a women. Her eyes were narrowed a mixture of anger and disappointment etched onto her face.

"You're drunk again," she said sternly. "Do you know what time it is?" she said.

But the man was not to be deterred, feeling emboldened by his drunken state, "Oh, spare me your righteous indignation, woman. I'm a king, and kings do what they want," before stumbling inside.

Despite the late hour, She meticulously prepares a plate of rice for her husband, but as he devours it like a wild beast, a storm begins to brew within him.

With a sudden flare of anger, he accuses the food of being cold and lashes out, striking the wife with a brutal slap that send her head crashing against the wall. The drunkard wrath knows no bounds as he begins to rain kicks upon her lifeless body, shouting obscenities and demanding, she get up.

But as the minutes tick by and there is no response from the woman, a sense of unease begins to creep over him. He begins to sweat profusely as he checks her pulse, only to realize with mounting horror that she is unresponsive. In a moment of rare clarity, he lifts her lifeless body and rushes to the nearest hospital, driven by a fear that he may have gone too far this time.

As he bursts into the hospital, all eyes turn to him. The air is charged with suspicion and fear as the hospital staff freezed in pulse, watching him warily.

But he is focused on one thing only, saving his wife. With a sense of urgency, he rushes to the front desk, where a doctor stands, calmly, waiting for his next patient.

"Doctor, please help her," the drunkard pleaded, his voice trembling with fear and sadness. "She is, my beloved wife, she's fallen down the steps. She's hurt, she's in pain, and I don't know what to do. Please, you have to help her.

The doctor looked at drunkard with a cold, hard gaze that made his heart sink. "Get lost," the doctor said in a voice that lacked any sympathy.

Please," he said, falling to his knees and grasping the doctor's feet. "She's my everything, my reason for living. Without her, I am nothing."

The doctor raised an eyebrow, looking skeptical. "Who is she and what is your relation with her? he asked , his tone measured.

"I've told you already," he said, his voice growing desperate. " He dug his pocket, pulling out a photograph. He thrust it towards the doctor, pointing to the image of the newly married couple, beaming with happiness.

"Look," he said, holding it out to the doctor. "This is my wife, and me. We were so happy, so in love. She's the only one who understands me, who sees the good in me. Please, you have to help her."

The doctor looked at the photograph, his expression unreadable. "The person in the photo is not you, and this is not your wife." said the doctor.

He felt a surge of anger boil inside him listening the doctor's words. He lunged forward, grabbing the doctor collar. The two orderlies rushed forward, pulling him back from the doctor.

"Let me go!" he roared. "How dare you dismiss my love for her like it means nothing? She's my wife, damn it! I'll do anything to save her!"

As he was pulled away, he caught a glimpse of himself in a mirror. And what he saw there made his blood run cold. He saw a strange, creepy man with irregularly grown hair and beard, wearing a green hospital gown. And there was a badge on his chest, labelling him as "patient Arjun."

He starred in horror at the stretcher where he thought his wife was lying. But when he saw the nurse sitting up, he realized then that he was the one in the hospital, not his wife, that it was just another trick of his mind. In that moment, the reality of his situation hit him like a ton of bricks. He was not a husband rushed to the aid of his wife. He was a patient in a mental hospital, trapped in a never ending cycle of madness and delusion.

But Arjun was not willing to accept his fate. As he was led back to his room, he fought against the orderlies, thrashing and struggling with all his might.

"I won't let you do this to me!" he roared. "I am arjun, and I refuse to be a prisoner in this place!"

The hospital staff rushed in, trying to subdue him with shock treatment, but it was no use. He was too strong, too determined. He wouldn't let them control him any longer.

In a final act of desperation, one of the staff members clubbed arjun on the back of the head, sending him spiraling into a deep coma.

As arjun lain in a coma, the medical staff attempted to reach his wife, with a frantic phone call. The phone rang loudly in her home, just as the doorbell began to sound with a shrill insistence. She, her mind clouded with a growing sense of unease, answered the door to find her mother, Raani, standing on the threshold, an angry scowl creasing her face.

"What took you so long to answer laxmi?" Raani snapped.

laxmi was taken aback, speechless in the face of her mother's sudden aggression. She simply turned and walked away, leaving raani to search for her granddaughter, chinnu on her own.

"Chinnu! Chinnu! "Raani called out, her voice growing more and more frantic with each passing moment.

Laxmis's thoughts muddled, pointed towards the bedroom. Raani when entered the bedroom, she was greeted with a horrifying sight, chinnu was tied to a chair, her hands and legs bound, her mouth gagged with duct pipe. The floor was wet with a pungent smell of urine.

The house was shocked in a pall of silence, broken only by the insistent ring of the phone. Laxmi answered it, her voice tight with apprehension. The news was grim ,her husband was in a coma and his condition was rapidly deteriorating.

Laxmi's mind racing as she hung up the phone. In the other room, raani still stood frozen, staring at her daughter with a mixture of horror and disbelief.

"What kind of monster are you?" Raani whispered, her voice barely audible. "What have you done to chinnu?"

laxmi's eyes narrowed, a cruel smile spreading across her face. "This little brat started to shout just like her father," she said, her voice cold and merciless. "Who's to blame if I did the same to her like I did with his father?"

Raani recoiled, aghast at the revelation. She could barely bring herself to look at her daughter, her mind grappling with the horror of what she had just heard.

And then, without another word, laxmi handed her mother a glass of water and left the house and went to the hospital. As she stood beside her comatose husband in the sterile hospital room, the reality of the situation began to sink in. The tears flowed down her cheeks, unchecked, and she wept inconsolably. The medical staff tried to comfort her, but their words fell on deaf ears. Eventually they left the room, granting the couple a moment of privacy in their grief.

Laxmi slowly raised herself up, wiping away her tears with trembling hands. She leaned in close to her husband's face, pressing a soft kiss to his forehead. In a voice just above a whisper, she spoke into his ear, "Say hello to your brother." with those chilling words, she removed his oxygen mask and walked out of the room without looking back.

CHAPTER SEVEN

THE U TURN

After listening the story narrated by my grandmother, it left me a felling frightened and uncertain. I stood silent for a moment, unsure of what to say , as my grandmother's words echoed in my mind. Just as my grandmother is about to continue with the story, my mother ,interrupts her and reveals a shocking revelation.

"Mother, the teacher didn't kiss arjun, she kissed surya," said my mother, leaving everyone stunned and confused.

"With this revelation, the entire story takes a sudden turn. I am shocked by the news and my mind is swirling with questions. What else has my grandmother been lying about? Why did my mother wait until now to reveal the truth?".

Revenge is the purest form emotion
- Mahabharatha

Printed by Libri Plureos GmbH in Hamburg,
Germany